# DEADWOOD *Shorts*

# Tequila & T/Lime

Ann Charles

Illustrated by C.S. Kunkle

Deadwood Shorts: Tequila & Time



Cover Design by Sharon Benton (www.q42designs.com)
Edited by Eilis Flynn (www.emsflynn.com)

E-book ISBN-13: 978-1-940364-49-0
Print ISBN-:13: 978-1-940364-48-3

Want to add some laughter, adventure, and spice to your life?
Check out all three of Ann Charles' mystery series:

Stop by for a visit to the Old West town of Deadwood, South Dakota—the Ann Charles version. This USA Today bestselling, multiple award-winning humorous mystery series is packed with quirky characters, nail-biting paranormal suspense, and spicy romance. Violet Parker will have to hang on tight and stick to her guns through the crazy adventures in store for her. Thank goodness she has a lot of gumption and help from her friends.

Welcome to the jungle—the steamy Maya jungle that is, filled with ancient ruins and deadly secrets. Quint Parker, renowned photojournalist (and lousy amateur detective), is in for a whirlwind of adventure and suspense as he and archaeologist, Dr. Angélica García, get tangled up in mysteries from the past and present at exotic dig sites. Loaded with action and laughs, along with all sorts of steamy heat, these two will keep you sweating along with them as they do their best to make it out of the jungle alive in every book.

A Jackrabbit Junction Mystery

Down here at the Dancing Winnebagos RV Park in Jackrabbit Junction, Arizona, Claire Morgan and her rabble-rousing sisters are really good at getting into trouble—BIG trouble (the land your butt in jail kind of trouble). This rowdy, laugh-aloud mystery series is packed with action, suspense, adventure, and relationship snafus. Full of colorful characters and twisted up plots, the stories of the Morgan sisters will keep you wondering what kind of a screwball mess they are going to land in next.

**For more information about Ann and her books, check out her website, as well as the reader reviews for her books on Amazon, Barnes & Noble, and Goodreads**

Dear Reader,

Tequila is a slippery devil.

I speak from experience. I've been a fan of the agave plant in its liquid form for many moons. So, when it came time to write another short story about some of the Deadwood crew, I naturally returned to the bottle to grease some tongues—theirs, not mine.

In this short story, Violet and Natalie volunteered, both of them more than willing to share some screen time in exchange for shots of tequila. As you can see, they are women after my own heart.

We all know that research is an important part of writing. Therefore, in an effort to make this Deadwood Short accurate, I sacrificed myself for the good of the story. One night, after my kids had gone to bed, I had my husband play bartender and line up a row of tequila shots, lime slices, and salt. After each shot, I recorded the outcome so that I could experience sliding down that slippery tequila slope along with Violet and Natalie.

It was a tough job, but someone had to do it.

I hope you enjoy the outcome of my research and share some laughs with me as Violet and Natalie hash out a few truths in "Tequila & Time." Truths that slip free only after a little oiling of their tongues.

Whatever your drink of choice, let's raise a glass to friendship and tequila—both of which come many times with side effects of wild laughter and bad decisions.

Thank you for hanging out yet again with the nutty characters living in my head.

Ann Charles

www.anncharles.com

*To Sister Wendy*

*You have given so much time and energy to help me on this wild ride.*

*Your spot-on marketing ideas, your excellent monkey-handling skills, and your continued willingness to learn and try new things have made working with you a fun adventure.*

*I've lost count of how many times we've shared liquor and laughter over the years (which I blame on all of the tequila, wine, and rum).*

*Thank you! This one is for you.*

# Also by Ann Charles

**Deadwood Mystery Series**
Nearly Departed in Deadwood (Book 1)
Optical Delusions in Deadwood (Book 2)
Dead Case in Deadwood (Book 3)
Better Off Dead in Deadwood (Book 4)
An Ex to Grind in Deadwood (Book 5)
Meanwhile, Back in Deadwood (Book 6)
A Wild Fright in Deadwood (Book 7)

**Short Stories from the Deadwood Mystery Series**
Deadwood Shorts: Seeing Trouble
Deadwood Shorts: Boot Points
Deadwood Shorts: Cold Flame

**Jackrabbit Junction Mystery Series**
Dance of the Winnebagos (Book 1)
Jackrabbit Junction Jitters (Book 2)
The Great Jackalope Stampede (Book 3)
The Rowdy Coyote Rumble (Book 4)
The Wild Turkey Tango (Novella 4.5)

**Goldwash Mystery Series (a future series)**
The Old Man's Back in Town (Short Story)

**Dig Site Mystery Series**
Look What the Wind Blew In (Book 1)

# Coming Next from Ann Charles

**Dig Site Mystery Series**
Make No Bones About It (Book 2)

**Deadwood Mystery Series**
Title TBA (Book 8)

# Acknowledgments

This is a short story, so this is going to be a short acknowledgment. Seems fitting, right?

Thank you to my husband, kids, family, friends, graphic artist, artist, editors, first-draft readers, local expert, world keeper, beta readers, promotion team, and mouthy cats. Thanks also to my brother, Clint, who loves me in spite of my inability to cook well.

Special thanks to my good author buddy, Jacquie Rogers, for writing back and forth with me while I was drunk from tequila shots. Next time you need to be here slamming them with me.

Thank you to all who support me and my books by reading them and laughing out loud about what's on the pages in front of spouses, friends, family, enemies, and complete strangers in crowded subways, trains, and elevators.

Many thanks to the libraries, bookstores, tourist shops, and other venues that help me by displaying or selling my books in your stores.

Finally, a big thanks to YOU for reading my books and supporting my addiction to storytelling. Without you, I would be in an insane asylum scratching these words on the walls with a spoon I stole from the cafeteria when the guards weren't looking.

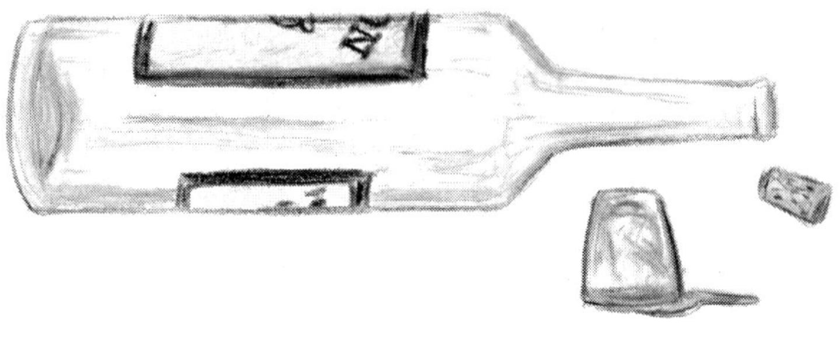

"The problem with the world is that everyone is a few drinks behind."

~Humphrey Bogart

# One Tequila

*The Purple Door Saloon*
*Deadwood, South Dakota*

In my three-plus decades of celebrating life's rainbows and dodging its shit-storms, I'd learned a valuable lesson—birthdays and underwear always went down easier with a shot of tequila.

Or four.

This evening was all about basking in the glow of my best friend's birthday candles and drinking to another year of breathing oxygen. Whether my underwear stayed on my hips later would be determined by a certain man with magic hands who had a tricky way of making my clothes fall off before I'd realized it.

"I have three words for you tonight, Nat." I grabbed the salt shaker and slid it across the scarred wooden table at our favorite drinking hole. "Lick, sip, and suck."

Natalie crossed her arms over her chest. With her thick brunette hair pulled back in a ponytail and only a layer of gloss coating her full lips, she looked like she was celebrating twenty-nine years rather than thirty-six. "Violet Parker, if you're going to try to pick me up, you need to do better than that."

Natalie and I had been sharing secrets and giggles since long before we'd sprouted boobs or daydreamed about boys and happily-ever-afters. I had a brand new pickup line ready to share with her. I'd just been waiting for the right moment.

"Do you like pirates, gorgeous?" I fought to keep from smiling. "Because I got a lot of seamen that wanna meet ya. Ayyy matey!" While she laughed, I added a gravelly, "Yaharrrr har har!"

"Oh, God. That reminds me of the architect who tried to pick me up last month at the Golden Sluice in Lead."

"An architect, huh?" I wiggled my eyebrows at her.

"Yeah." She grimaced. "He said he'd erected a monument in his pants just for me."

We were still snickering when the waitress stopped by our table. "What can I get you two?"

"Four tequila shots each with lime wedges and some of that kosher salt you keep behind the bar, please," I ordered. "It's time to get this birthday girl completely wasted."

After the waitress left us alone, Natalie raised one eyebrow. "*Four* shots, Vi?"

"Yes, four." I sat back in the booth seat, pulling my arms free from the sleeves of my red pea coat. It had taken a good ten minutes to warm up after hiking several blocks from work in the freezing winds blasting through Deadwood Gulch. "A shot for each decade we've been friends plus one to grow on."

"Fine, but who's going to carry us home when we're done?"

"Doc said he'd swing by after the poker game is done."

Doc Nyce, aka Mr. Magic Hands, was the one guy on the planet allowed to see me naked. Earlier on the phone, he'd made me promise that Natalie and I wouldn't leave the bar until he showed up to haul us out and make sure we made it home in one drunken piece.

"I thought the guys' poker night was on Wednesdays," Natalie said.

"It usually is, but Detective Cooper's been so stressed lately about all of the murder case files on his desk that Doc figured a night of drowning in whiskey, cards, and trash talk would provide a much needed distraction."

Natalie smirked. "Poor Coop. He'll probably get his ass kicked by your boyfriend to boot."

I rubbed my palms together, warming them. "Oddly enough, I have a feeling Cooper enjoys the rivalry with Doc."

"A budding *bromance*, maybe? That's sweet."

"I wouldn't say that in front of Cooper. He's all horns and teeth lately, perpetually pissed off and snorting."

Natalie waved me off. "Coop's an alpha male with a super-sized order of testosterone. Underneath that sandpaper hide and those serrated teeth is a nice guy in need of a few good friends."

"Oh, really? And you know this because you're now

older and wiser than me?" My thirty-sixth birthday wouldn't swing around for another few months.

"Well, that's a given." She grinned at me. "But I've also been around the block with the male species enough to know a good-looking dickwad from a kind-hearted crabby pants."

"Is this the new enlightened you speaking? The one who has been on sabbatical from men long enough now to see beyond big biceps and broad shoulders and listen to what's spilling from their lips?"

"Partly." She laced her fingers together on the table. "It's also the me who is coming up on forty and accepting that I'm probably never going to find Prince Charming, let alone get to live the dream."

"The dream being what? To buy a fancy sports car and take lavish vacations that end with sex on moonlit beaches with smoking-hot strangers?"

"Since when do you like moonlit beaches? I thought you didn't enjoy getting sand in all of your cracks and crevices."

"Actually, it's the sand fleas that give me the heebie-jeebies." I scratched my neck. "I get all itchy just thinking about them."

"I don't need the fancy car or the lavish vacations."

"What's the dream then? And don't tell me it involves having kids, because you've seen my life with twins. It's full of dirty laundry, snotty noses, lots of yelling, and an ornery chicken."

"True, but your heart is full."

She had me there. "Full, yes, but also worn, bruised, and ragged in several spots, and I'm only a decade into this parenthood business."

"Don't give me your sob story. I know you love those two kids with every cell in your body. I was there when they were born, remember? I saw the way your face lit up the first time you saw them."

I drew some invisible hearts on the table with my finger. "Of course I love my kids, but being a parent is scary and stressful as hell. Children change the way you see your surroundings. From the moment they popped out of my womb, I started noticing all of the things in this world that could injure, maim, or kill them. Paper airplanes can take out an eyeball, you know."

"Yes, I do know, Ms. Paranoid Nutjob, because you warn the kids and me about it every time we make paper airplanes."

"Takes a nutjob to know one."

The jukebox came to life with The Eagles telling us to "Take It Easy," which seemed appropriate for tonight's celebration.

"Where are your two bundles of joy this evening?" Natalie asked. "I swung by your aunt's place to drop off my overnight bag and see if you were home from work yet, but the place was dark."

"Aunt Zoe took them to some kids' movie in Spearfish."

"Did you bribe her?"

"I didn't need to. She loves hanging out with the little turkeys, says they keep her feeling young and feisty. I tell her they keep her crazy, like me, but she just doesn't realize it yet."

"Zoe's only in her fifties." Natalie leaned forward, a sparkle in her eye. "I know someone who'd like to make her feel young and feisty again, along with all sorts of other good feelings."

"Me, too." Unfortunately, Aunt Zoe was still resisting a certain Deadwood fire captain's attempts to charm away her loneliness. "But Reid's too busy playing poker with Doc and Cooper tonight to risk Aunt Zoe's wrath … or her shotgun."

"Who's their fourth?"

"Harvey, I think." My part-time bodyguard had told me earlier he'd cancelled a hot date with a sizzling old flame to help cheer up his nephew. "They're having the game at Doc's house and Harvey volunteered to provide *hors d'oeuvres.*" If it hadn't been for Natalie's birthday, I might have crashed the game just to steal some food. Betty Crocker had nothing on the horny goat.

The waitress brought our tequilas, lining the shot glasses up in front of us. She placed a plate with lime wedges in the center of the table along with a bowl of kosher salt.

As soon as she left, Natalie reached for one of her shots but I slapped her hand away. "Not yet, birthday girl. We're going to play a game tonight."

"Quarters?"

"No way. It grosses me out to drink anything after a dirty coin has soaked in it."

"Jeez, you're such a mom." She leaned back in the seat. "What's the game?"

"We each have to tell something about our past that the other doesn't know."

She scoffed. "That's going to be too hard. I've known you almost as long as I've known myself."

That was true. I rubbed my chin for a couple of seconds in thought. "Okay, how about I ask you a question and you can either answer it or take a drink instead?"

"Like Truth or Dare only we can drink instead of take the dare?"

"Yes, truth or drink."

"You don't want to do any dares, huh?"

"I only had a protein bar and a piece of cheese before leaving work tonight. Four shots on a half-empty stomach means trouble when it comes to taking dares. I don't want to end up in jail like last time."

"Good point. I'm getting too old for the hoosegow."

Natalie held her closed fist out. "Shall we rock-paper-scissors for who goes first?"

I pushed her fist away. "It's your big night. You start."

It took her a handful of seconds to come up with a question, during which the Eagles wrapped up their Winslow, Arizona, tribute. George Thorogood and the Destroyers started cranking out "Bad to the Bone," filling the bar with guitar riffs that had me nodding along.

"Truth or drink?" Natalie interrupted my impression of George's raspy voice. "When you found out you were pregnant, did you ever contemplate giving up the kids for adoption? And be honest."

I thought we'd discussed this once before, but maybe it was Aunt Zoe who had asked me that after I'd threatened to send Addy and Layne to boarding school in Siberia for throwing my parents' old yard darts at each other during a fight. Talk about putting an eye out … or worse! "That's an easy one. I'll tell the truth, which is no."

"Really? Even after you found out you were pregnant with not one baby but two, and their jackass father wanted nothing to do with them?"

"Especially after learning both of those things. Those babies were mine. You know how I've always taken my responsibilities seriously."

"Oh, fuzz balls. You're talking about that stupid peacock, aren't you?"

"Francis McFowl was not stupid. He'd gotten lost during a night of scary thunderstorms and needed help getting his bearings." I'd found the poor peacock in our backyard the next morning with several of his beautiful feathers bent or broken.

"And you wonder where your daughter gets it."

I pointed at Natalie. "Unlike Addy and her damned chicken, I didn't keep Francis. I found him a home."

"Sure, after making the farmer sign a contract that he

wouldn't hurt a single one of Francis's tail feathers."

"It was my duty to see to his well-being."

"So you're saying those two babies were your duty, too?"

I pondered that for a few guitar riffs, wanting to be completely honest with Natalie. "Maybe it started out that way, but from the moment I felt them wiggling inside my belly, I fell in love. I knew deep down that come hell or high water," or psychotic killers and ax-wielding juggernauts, "I was going to do everything I could to protect them. The absence of a father meant they'd need me even more."

"See." She pointed back at me. "That's the 'dream' I'm

talking about. Unless I decide to visit a sperm bank, experiencing that kind of love is not in my future."

I chewed on my lower lip, trying to come up with a way to help temporarily fill the empty corner in her heart that she'd apparently reserved for kids. All I could think of was, "Don't give up yet," which sounded one hundred percent, grade-A lame.

She rolled her eyes at me. "Shut up, Dr. Phil. It's your turn to ask me a question."

There was something that I'd wondered for a while, but I hadn't been sure how to ask it. Now with tequila on the table between us, it seemed like a good time to go for it. "Truth or drink? Have you ever analyzed your past to figure out why you keep choosing asshole boyfriends who end up screwing around on you?"

She stared at me for several seconds, her gaze narrowed and wary, bordering on defensive. Then she sighed and laced her fingers behind her head. "Wow, you're not tiptoeing around tonight, are you?"

I shrugged. "Life's too short. You're already thirty-six. If I dillydally much longer, we'll both be dead. Besides, Doc said they'd be wrapping up earlier than usual since Reid and Cooper both have to be at work at the ass-crack of dawn, so we only have two hours left, maybe three."

She reached for a shot, frowning down at it.

"Come on, Nat. Don't tell me you're going to wimp out on my first question and take the drink."

Her eyes lifted to mine, her forehead furrowing. "I'm not sure I want to dig that deep into my psyche tonight. It is my birthday, you know. This is supposed to be fun."

"So make it fun. I'm not looking for something to share on talk shows here. Just tell me, was there some jackass in high school who treated you like shit and beat up your self-esteem? A douchebag you didn't want to tell me about?"

She shook her head.

"Someone who teased you about something when we were younger? Your chest, maybe?" Boys could be such dicks in junior high.

She continued shaking her head. "My boobs were never a source of harassment."

"Your lips then?"

"What's wrong with my lips?"

"You know it took you a couple of years to grow into those baby inner tubes."

She blew a kiss at me with her full, beautiful lips.

"Was it that shithead, Kenny Kirkindale? Wasn't he the one who called you 'Steven Tyler' every time you came down to Rapid to go to a football game with me?" Natalie had gone to high school up in Lead, but she'd spent almost every weekend down in Rapid City with me or her cousins.

She still shook her head.

"Because if it was Kenny and his stupid mouth, you know he had the hots for you, right? He wrote something nasty in the boys' locker room about what he wanted you to do with your big lips."

"Oh, yuck." She fake gagged. "How do you know about what he wrote? When were you in the boys' locker room?"

"Quint told me." My older brother had been in high school at the time. "He roughed up Kenny for writing that shit about you and made him scour it off with steel wool."

She grinned, resting her chin on the heel of her palm. "I love your brother. It's too bad I adopted him as my own long before he filled out in all of the right places." A small shadow passed behind her eyes, dimming her smile for a moment, and then it was gone.

"So, are you going to tell the truth on this or drink?"

"I thought I was telling the truth."

"You're half-assing it. Come on, Nat, it's my first question. Give me something here."

"Okay. Yes, I have thought about why I keep falling for

no-good, cheating bastards." She nudged the shot glass away. "I've thought about it a lot, especially right after catching Doc and you together that night at Mudder Brothers."

I winced, fighting the urge to slink down in my seat.

Early this last summer, Natalie had staked a claim on Doc while I was sidetracked by Wolfgang Hessler, a handsome blond jeweler who'd hired me to sell his house. But then I'd run into Doc and been knocked on my ass—literally. At first, I'd thought Doc was half a bubble off plumb and Wolfgang was my dream come true. In the end, Wolfgang was my worst nightmare and Doc's level-headedness saved my bacon. So, rather than tell Natalie that I had an unshakable crush for the guy starring in her wedding fantasies, I jumped her claim, stealing Doc out from under her.

As crappy friends went, I ranked as the top turd.

With my cheeks a shade redder due to my reckless past behavior, I remained top side and waited her out. "And?"

"I have a great dad and brother."

Where was this going? "Yes, you do. Although your brother did shoot me in the butt with a BB gun once."

"You're lucky it was only once. He'd shot me three times before I got hold of that damned gun and broke it in two. But other than his BB fetish, you have to admit he's grown up to be a sweetheart."

I had no argument there. "So what's your point about your dad and brother?"

She tucked a loose strand of hair behind her ear. "I grew up thinking that all men were good guys like them. Honest. Warm-hearted. True blue." She smirked. "Well, we both know now how silly that belief is, right? I mean I'm sure there are decent guys around, like Doc for one, but I have yet to find one. I'm beginning to think I'd have better luck hunting snipe."

"So let me get this straight," I said, running my finger around the rim of one of the shot glasses. "Rather than your relationship problems stemming from a *lack* of positive male role models in your life, it's due to an abundance of them in your early years."

"Bingo, babe." She touched her finger to her nose. "Along with the fact that I'm a fixer."

"A fixer?"

"Yep. I like to fix things that are broken. Why do you think I carry around a bunch of tools in my pickup?"

"Because you like to put the hammer down like Thor." I pantomimed swinging a hammer down on the table.

"Oh my God. Are you for real? You need to fire whoever is writing your one-liners tonight."

"What? I thought I was pretty clever."

"Pretty? Yes, you are, especially in that shade of blue. But clever? I don't know if you're pulling that off yet tonight, but give me a few shots of tequila and I'll probably think you're freaking brilliant." She dodged the bar napkin I wadded up and threw at her. "I'm a fixer, Vi. Think about all of the times I've tried to fix your life."

True. She'd fixed my problems more times than I could count. "Fortunately for you, I'm an ace at screwing up."

She smiled too easily at that, dang it. "I've tried to fix many of the men I've dated, too, especially the select few I've actually allowed in my bed. But since I've stopped looking for Mr. Right and focused on enjoying my life sans men, I've come to realize the error of my ways."

"And now that you've figured this out about yourself, are you ready to return to your search for Mr. Right?"

I asked on behalf of a certain detective on the Deadwood police force who couldn't seem to take his eyes off her whenever she came near. Cooper and Natalie had a history, about which I'd only semi-recently learned. So far, I'd heard bits and pieces from Natalie about something that had occurred in this very bar years back involving the two of them—something fiery with passion that had ended in a burning rejection, leaving Natalie's pride scarred. Tonight with the help of tequila, I hoped to learn exactly what went down so I could make a decision whether or not to tell my best friend that Cooper seemed to have changed his mind about sharing more than friendly fire with her.

"No way. I'm sick of having my heart broken. There's no way I'm going to open my tool chest again."

"Never?"

"Never say never." She shrugged. "But I'll tell you one thing. No matter how attracted I am to a guy, if he's damaged I'm keeping my fixer-upper tools packed away and running like hell in the other direction."

That was bad news for Cooper. The detective was one big stress-fractured mess. Part of me felt bad for the bristly bossy pants, but another part was dancing a jig. I wasn't thrilled with the idea of the detective burrowing even deeper into my private life. Cooper was already rooming with my boyfriend while I worked on selling his house. Hooking up with my best friend would turn my life into one of those damned cop dramas 24/7.

"Was that truth good enough?" she asked me.

I gave her a thumbs-up. "Your turn."

She leaned forward, her gaze narrowing again. "Truth or drink? When did you have sex with Doc for the first time?"

Oh, shazbot! While I'd come clean to her that Doc and I had started dating when I was supposed to be keeping my hands off of him, I'd not really given her any of the finer details on how much of a man-stealing, back-stabbing best friend I'd been.

I opened my mouth to tell her the truth, but then reached for the salt instead. "Drink."

I sprinkled salt on the back of my hand, licked it, and tossed back the shot of tequila. It went down a little bumpy with a fiery burn at the end. I stuck one of the lime wedges in my mouth and sucked, smiling around the rind at her in spite of the sour fruit.

She stared at me with a hard glint for a few seconds, but then the corners of her eyes creased. "You big chicken."

I removed the lime. "Bok bok bok," I clucked.

"You know I've forgiven you for claim jumping, right?"

"Bok bok."

"I know full well that you and Doc were doing the wild thing behind my back, so there's no need to deny it."

"Bok."

"You're such a cluck-head," she said with a wide grin. "Your turn, Chicken Little."

I thought for a moment while playing with the empty shot glass, debating on digging into that night she had with Cooper, but then I veered in a different direction. "Truth or drink? How many men have you actually had sex with?"

She snorted. "Why does that matter?"

"Truth or drink, girlfriend? How many for real?" Something she'd said a few weeks back on the phone had gotten me to wondering if she was as wild and willing to hop in the sack as I'd always thought.

"When you say *sex*, what do you mean?" she asked.

"I mean the actual full-on mating process, as in how babies are made."

"Truth." She held up one hand with all five fingers out.

Only five? "No way!"

"Yes way!" Her indignant tone matched my level of disbelief.

"Come on, your dance card reads like the white pages."

"You didn't ask how many men I've dated or kissed, only how many I've had sex with. There's a *big* difference."

"You're telling me that you've dated a ton of guys but only experienced actual penetration with five."

She wrinkled her upper lip. "Do you have to use the

word *penetration*? It sort of takes the fun out of the whole shebang. Pun intended."

"*She-bang?* Talk about me and my lousy one-liners. No more puns from you until I'm officially drunk."

"Whatever. You have my truth."

I sat back, shaking my head. "But all of this time you acted like you were a sailor on shore leave."

"No, all of this time you assumed that the guys I dated ended up in my bed."

"Wow." I really did slink down in my seat then. "I truly suck." I scratched my head. "Why do you keep me as a friend?"

"Because I signed a contract with your parents when I was four."

"Well, thank God for their foresight then." I let out a laugh of disbelief. "Do you realize I've slept with more guys than you?"

"You tramp." Her smile took the sting out of her words.

"Make that one more guy than you," and that *one* was Doc, who I hoped to be the last in the lineup. "But you've kissed more, you hussy."

She blew me an air kiss. "I have to use these big lips for something besides sinking ships."

I toyed with my empty shot glass. "I guess I was living vicariously, since I was at home on weekend nights with my two kids while you were out at bars. I saw you as having a wild-woman life without even asking if it was true."

"Don't feel bad. I never corrected your assumption."

I frowned at her. "Why didn't you?"

"Because it made up for my not having someone waiting at home each night. If I were living this pretend life full of hot guys and crazy times, it didn't feel so empty."

I reached over and pushed a full shot glass her way. "That truth is worth a drink, hot lips. Lick, sip, and suck."

# Two Tequila

*One trip to the ladies' room later …*

"Okay," I said, settling back into my booth seat. "One tequila down, three to go. Whose turn is it?"

My lips were beginning to tingle from that first shot and my chest was warm from the tequila's fiery trip down my esophagus, but otherwise I could still chew bubblegum while tying my shoes—that was if I had gum and weren't wearing boots.

"You asked the last nosy-nelly question about my sex life," Natalie reminded me, "so it's my turn."

I leveled my shoulders and prepared for her next torpedo. "Let's have it."

"Truth or drink? Did you ever kiss my brother?"

I flinched. "Ewww. Truth. No way."

"You don't need to say that like he's carrying the plague."

"It's not that. Your brother is hot, totally, trust me. But I've known him since he was in diapers. In fact, I think I helped change his diaper once."

"If what disgusts you on the kissing front are his droopy diapers, I can assure you that at almost thirty-three years of age he's now grown out of that stage."

I laughed louder than normal, drawing several stares from the smattering of patrons at the nearby tables. *Sorry*, I mouthed to them and pointed at the empty shot glass.

Back to Nat, I explained, "Sucking face with your little brother would be like kissing Quint, and I know they say incest is best and I should put my family to the test, but I was never good at taking tests. The anxiety messes with my head."

"Well, I'm glad to hear that—the lack of incest in your world, I mean, not the bit about testing."

"My turn. Truth or drink? Did you ever kiss *my* brother?" I tossed her question back in her court.

"Quint?"

"Unless you know of another male who shares parents with me, then yes. Quint Parker. My brother. Did you kiss him?"

She hesitated.

My jaw dropped. "You didn't!"

"Back when I was in junior high and he was in high school," she started.

"Oh my God!" I covered my mouth with my hand, adding through my fingers, "I can't believe you kissed my brother!"

"I didn't kiss him."

My hand dropped. "Well then what the hell?"

"If you'd let me finish with my 'truth,' Chatty Cathy, you'd hear that I *thought* about kissing him, that's all. Nothing more. And he has no idea it even crossed my mind."

"You sure about that?"

"Positive. He's always treated me as if I was his little sister, but for about a week in seventh grade I wondered what it would be like to kiss him."

I scrunched up my face. "Why?"

"Because I saw him kissing Jenny Appellino under the bleachers during a football game."

"Jenny Appellino?" I wrinkled my upper lip. "Ick. I couldn't stand that snobby bitch. I didn't know Quint dated her."

"I don't think they dated, he just kissed her."

"Why would he bother with her? She wasn't really his type." Quint was never into bubbly girls. He had a thing for the brainy babes.

"She might not have been his type, but with that killer rack and the little cheerleading skirt, she was a real hot commodity for a while. Remember the way she'd jump around wearing her tight sweater during the football games? Half of the guys in your school were too busy watching her boobs bounce to notice that they'd won the division championship."

I growled in my throat. "She always made fun of my hair."

"I'll tell you what. The next time I run into Jenny, I'll put gum in her hair and tell her you send your love."

"You're trying to fix my problems again."

"Fine, you put gum in her hair and I'll kiss her older brother."

"Isn't he in jail?"

"I heard he's out on parole."

"You'd kiss a parolee for me? What a great friend."

"Promise me you won't tell Quint about my week-long crush. I don't want to make things weird between us over something so silly."

"Of course I won't. Tonight's tequila talk is between you and me, hot lips." I frowned at her. "I'm glad you never actually kissed Quint. That would be weird."

"No weirder than you changing my brother's diaper and now thinking he's hot."

"Good point." I held up my empty shot glass for a toast. "No more brother talk."

"Hear, hear." She clinked her shot glass against mine. "My turn. Truth or drink? That night Doc and I went on that double date with you and—"

"It wasn't a double date," I interrupted.

She had dragged Doc down to Rapid City on the false assumption that I'd needed rescuing from a shared dinner with a guy who was now my co-worker. Such was life in a small town.

"Yes, it was," she insisted. "You two were on a dinner date and then—"

"I wasn't on a date with him."

"And then," she continued, talking over me, "I showed up with Doc and we joined you both for dinner and drinks."

"It wasn't a date for me. We were just two Star Trek fans sharing stories over food."

"It was a date, Violet."

"And Doc and you weren't officially on a date either," I added. "You'd hijacked him into coming to my rescue. He had no idea that I was actually there with another guy, or he wouldn't have gone."

I could clearly remember his squinty eyes and tight jaw when he walked up to our table that evening.

"Anyway." She gave me a shut it pinch. "That night, you disappeared during our appetizers."

"I had to use the bathroom."

"And you didn't come back for a long time."

"Were you timing me?"

She held up her hand. "Doc disappeared at almost the same time, claiming a need to use the restroom, too."

"We're all human. Having to go to the bathroom is a natural thing."

"Truth or drink? Did you two screw around in one of the bathrooms while your *date* and I waited for you to come back?"

Technically, no, we didn't screw around in the bathroom. We screwed around in the darkened, empty banquet room located beyond the bathrooms.

I smiled sheepishly and lifted a shot glass. "Drink."

She watched me with a gunslinger glare as I licked, sipped, and sucked. When I finished pounding on my sternum after the tequila train burned its way down, I blew out a breath. "That's some good stuff."

"You're not going to tell me anything about the early days between Doc and you, are you?"

"You can read it in my autobiography when we're little old raisins."

A fleeting wave of dizziness made my head list to the side. I probably should have ordered a burger from the waitress with my tequila shots, something to soak up the liquor. Feeling the need for a kickstand, I leaned my elbows on the table. "My turn to play." That last word came out a little wet.

"You're starting to spit when you talk."

I blew a raspberry at her.

She used a drink napkin to dab off her arm. "I can see there will be no fixing you tonight."

"Nope. You might as well join me."

"What's your question then, you trampy boozehound?"

"Truth or drink? Do you think Detective Cooper is good looking?"

She scoffed. "That's easy. Truth. Yes."

"Aha!"

"Aha what? I've told you that before. Remember? We had a bit of fun here years back, sharing a drink." She looked down at her hands. "And then some."

"Did you kiss him?"

"Yes." Her gaze met mine. "I told you that, too."

"Did you do anything else?"

Her eyes shuttered, closing me out. "He rejected me, remember? Said he's not into local girls."

I might be two shots deep in tequila, but I was sober enough to know that she didn't exactly answer my question.

I opened my mouth to interrogate further, but she stood.

"Let's go play some pool."

"Wait!" I pointed at the shots. "We're not done yet."

"Fine." She sank back into the booth seat. "Truth or drink? What's more satisfying, selling a house or killing a monster?"

I glanced around the bar, making sure nobody else was listening. "Killing a monster?" I asked in a hushed voice.

She leaned forward, whispering back. "You heard me."

I frowned, uncomfortable speaking out loud about my other, darker role in life that involved slaying nasty agitators that were out to stir up trouble. It was a heroic role that pinched in some places and chafed in others, not to mention the damned cape, which was too long and kept getting caught under my heels. I had yet to get a handle on who I was supposed to remove and how. I wasn't even going to touch on the *why* part.

"Are you talking about the big albino-looking dude at the funeral parlor?" I asked.

"And the others. Truth or drink, Ms. Executioner?"

I winced at the sound of my *other* name. "Don't call me that here."

"Quit stalling, Violet."

"Okay, okay." I hadn't really ever compared the two before. "Truth, I guess."

"All right, let me hear it."

"Well, I like making a sale because I need money to support my kids."

"I didn't ask what you liked, I asked what was more satisfying."

"Sex is the most satisfying." I tried to derail her.

"That wasn't one of the options and you know it."

I closed my eyes for a moment, trying my answer on for size before saying it.

Killing was wrong. I'd been taught to be kind and

loving and nurturing since birth.

Killing was violent. Besides my daydreams about maiming the kids' piece of shit father and maybe a bossy detective or two, I really wasn't a violent person. Even when my sister, the bitch from hell, had poked me with a sharp stick, making me bleed, I'd kept my head and hadn't lashed out in return.

Killing was not accepted in society. Only psychopaths and lunatics took lives without remorse. Rational single mothers who were members of the Parent-Teacher Organization didn't jam sharp metal objects into living beings.

But said beings were evil, hurting innocent people, and as my Aunt Zoe had told me after informing me of my real purpose on Earth, someone had to take out the garbage in this town.

With a nod, I opened my eyes. "Killing is the most satisfying."

"I knew it!" She leaned over the table, wiggling her finger for me to come closer. When I did, she asked, "Does it wind you up the same as sex?"

"Noooo," I said. "Sex is better. At least with Doc." Shoot, that detail wasn't supposed to slip out.

She pulled back, waving her hand in her front of her face. "Wow! You smell like you marinated your tongue in tequila."

I stuck my marinated tongue out at her. "If you'd stop answering my questions with the truth and drink with me, you wouldn't smell it."

"Ask me something I don't want to tell you."

"Okay. Truth or drink? When you and Cooper were getting good and friendly that night years ago, did you let him touch you anywhere in the red zone?"

"What is your fascination with Cooper tonight?"

"I'm just trying to get the story straight."

"I've told you the story, we had some fun and then he rejected me because I'm a local girl. The End."

"No, it's not."

"What does that mean?"

Oops, I wasn't supposed to let that secret out of the bag. "I mean, I don't think that's the end. I suspect there is more you aren't telling me for some reason."

She frowned in reply.

"Truth or drink, Nat? Was there red-zone touching from him or not?"

She stared over at the pool table for a few breaths, and then she turned back and grabbed a pinch of salt. "Drink." She followed the salt with tequila and lime, setting her shot glass down hard. "He rejected me," she said when her pucker face cleared up. "Like I told you before, 'end of story.' Now let's go hit some pool balls around before I'm too drunk to beat your sorry ass."

# Three Tequila

*Ten minutes later over at the pool table …*

"I just don't understand why you won't come clean about what happened that night with Cooper." I frowned across the table at Natalie, who was chalking up her pool cue.

I'd swung by the jukebox on my way to the pool table and popped some quarters in to keep the tunes cranking, selecting some oldies but goodies to keep us company as we played. Currently, Boston was singing about having "More Than a Feeling." I could relate, being pretty damned certain deep in my gut that Natalie was hiding something about Cooper.

She set the chalk on the side of the table. "Yeah, well, I don't understand why you're not telling me what really happened between Doc and you either."

We'd reached a deadlock, it appeared. I leaned on the edge of the pool table. That second tequila still had me heated up from my throat to my stomach. Its lingering effects added a slight blur to everything in the Purple Door Saloon—from the stained-glass pool table chandelier to the flashing colors on the jukebox to the blur of patrons and wait staff moving here and there. I could feel my eyes move as I looked around, a sure sign that I was on my way to numb lips soon.

"Whose turn is it, anyway?" I asked.

"To shoot or ask questions?"

"Ask questions. I'm not so drunk that I can't keep up with the table play."

"Not yet anyway." She hit the cue ball into the racked balls, sinking the twelve ball and three ball. "I'll let you pick."

"The next question?"

"No, stripes or solids."

"Stripes," I said. "Always. You know my issue with solids."

She smirked, shaking her head at me. "Truth or drink? Do you enjoy looking at the dead bodies Coop and Detective Hawke show you?"

"Now why in the world would I enjoy looking at dead bodies?"

"I'm just checking to see how much this new executioner gig has affected your moral compass." She lined up her next shot. "Five ball in the corner."

"My moral compass is still pointing north when appropriate."

"Did you actually answer my question?" She sank the ball.

"No, I do not enjoy looking at dead bodies no matter how many times Cooper and Hawke make me. I still cringe and wince and sometimes even gag a little."

"That's good to hear." She walked around the table, sizing things up. "What's your next question for me?"

"Truth or drink? Who's better with a tool, you or Claire?"

Claire Morgan was Natalie's cousin. I'd grown up in the house next to the Morgan family down in Rapid City, which is how I came to meet Nat at such a young age. Claire and Natalie both followed in their grandfather's footsteps, swinging a hammer for a living. Whereas Claire had taken a shitload of college classes without ever quite landing a degree in addition to working with her hands, Natalie had focused solely on furthering her tool-toting career.

"Truth," Natalie said. "Claire is better. I have to study to learn certain building techniques. Her skill with her hands is innate." She leaned over the table. "Seven ball in the side."

I watched her sink the pool ball with ease. I might as well hang up my pool cue. Natalie wasn't drunk enough yet for me to even have a chance at getting a single shot. She would run the table in no time.

"Truth or drink?" she asked, coming around to join me. "Did you have any idea this was in your bloodline?"

"You mean my love for the Ramones?" I asked, bobbing my head along with "I Wanna Be Sedated," which was now blasting from the jukebox.

"You only ever listen to this song by them."

"Still, I love it."

"You know what I mean. Don't make me ask again."

"Truth. I had no idea this was in my bloodline. It wasn't until after I moved up here and started having nightmares and visions and all kinds of crazy experiences that I even realized I was anything other than a dud."

"You are far from a dud, babycakes." She sank the one ball without calling it.

"Hey, you forgot to call it. My turn."

She shrugged. "I was getting tired of playing alone."

"Whatever, show-off. Get out of my way." I hip bumped her to the side.

As I sized up the playing field, she leaned back against the wall. "You know you need to actually touch the cue tip to the ball in order for them to move across the felt. Or have you now developed the ability to move balls with your mind alone?"

"Truth or drink, mouth? Did you go all the way with Jeff Wymonds back in high school?" I pointed at the thirteen ball. "I'm putting that pretty lady in the far left corner."

"You sure you can handle that one?"

"Just answer the question."

"Truth. No."

I looked up from lining up the pool cue. "I thought you said something once about screwing around in the backseat with him."

"I let him get to second base, sure, but he had football on the brain."

"What's that mean? He left you to go play a game?"

"No, there was a game on the radio when we were screwing around and he was so distracted that he couldn't get his quarterback up off the bench, if you get my meaning."

I didn't think Jeff had that problem these days, at least not the way he made it sound. "Good."

"You don't want me to have had sex with Jeff? He used to be super good looking back in high school and had that whole small-town football hero thing going for him."

"I'd prefer you weren't one of the girls he bonked in school—his words, not mine. I don't think I could handle listening to his sordid tale of the deflowering of my best friend."

"Ah, aren't you sweet. You really do like me." She

pointed her pool cue at the table. "Are you going to take that shot sometime before I die?"

I nailed the thirteen ball, sinking it. "Happy?"

"Not yet, but after this third tequila I will be." She took a sip. When I protested, she held up her finger. "Just a sip to wet my big, inner-tube lips."

I rounded the table, lining up the fifteen ball, which I informed her was destined to end up in the side pocket.

She scoffed. "That's an easy one. Question time. Truth or drink? Do you think this will be the end of us?"

"You mean this pool game?"

"No, spaz, this executioner shit and all it entails."

Oh, that. Still, I played dumb. "The end of our friendship?"

That earned me a scowl. "Are you being dense on purpose?"

"Hey, I'm two tequilas to the wind here. You need to spell it out for me."

"You suck at spelling."

"B-I-T-E-M-E." I took the shot, but the damned fifteen ball bounced off the corner of the cushion.

Natalie laughed. "That's what you get for trying to spell and shoot at the same time." She came around and nudged me out of the way. "Now, truth or drink? Do you think your new job is hazardous to our health, meaning mine, Doc's, Harvey's, etc.?"

I sat down on a tall stool at one of the bar tables near the wall, or more like fell onto the stool. The weight of her question and the fear the answer invoked deep in my gut made my knees want to give way. "I hope not."

"Do I hear a *but* in there?" She leaned her hip against the pool table, her focus on me, not the balls.

"*But* I don't really know the answer. It certainly didn't end well for the last executioner and her family."

The bloodbath that had ended her reign as the town's

trash cleaner-upper still haunted my nightmares.

"Yeah, but you told me once that your Aunt Zoe said what happened to the last executioner may not happen to you. That nothing is certain in this game."

"True, but Prudence was a better executioner than I am."

"Says who?"

"Prudence." Or rather her ghost.

"She was a narcissistic killer."

"Maybe. But look at all of her trophy teeth." Prudence had liked to play tooth fairy with her prey. I recoiled at just the thought of sticking my hand in some stranger's mouth, let alone yanking out their teeth.

"Did she work alone?" Natalie asked.

"I think so."

"There you go."

"Where am I going?"

"You have a team." She pointed her pool cue at me. "You aren't fighting alone. The team will make you stronger than she was."

"I'm putting all of your lives in danger."

"If we didn't want to play in your sandbox, Vi, we wouldn't be here."

"Maybe, but you don't know what's hiding under the sand."

"Neither do you." She called her shot and then took it. The two ball fell into its designated pocket. "You're up."

"You made the shot."

"I mean with questions."

"Oh. Okay." I blinked. It took some concentration to lower and lift my lids. The tequila was working its magic, taking the sharp edge off the truths I was telling, making it easier for them to slide off my tongue and slip out through my lips. "Truth or drink? That night with Cooper here at the bar, did *you* touch him in the red zone?"

She didn't even hesitate, grabbing her shot glass and tossing it back, skipping the salt and lime entirely. "Drink," she said after setting the shot glass down.

"Come on," I berated. "Can't you just give me a few minor details?"

"You're not asking for minor details."

I stared at her, trying to read if she was avoiding answering out of stubbornness, or if there was something deeper that had hurt her more than his rejection. Something she was hiding. "How'd that last one go down?"

She grinned. "Smooth as turpentine."

"Are you afraid to answer my questions because Cooper will arrest you for telling on him?"

"No."

"Did you perform some secret blood pact with him that night?"

"No."

"Then what's with making it such a big secret?"

"Why are you making it such a big deal? What's done is done. I've moved on. He's moved on. Life has moved on. So should we here tonight."

Only Cooper hadn't moved on, and the more she held out on me, the more I was dying to hear the truth so I could figure out why she was trying to keep it hidden.

"Fine!" I growled. "Just shoot, would you?"

She aimed, shot, and missed.

We both stared at the pool table in surprise.

I finally grasped the situation. "You missed."

"I know."

"How come?"

"Because I've downed three tequila shots."

I grinned, sliding off my chair and floating over to the pool table. "Move over then, lush, and watch me kick your hiney."

"Oh yeah, trash talker?" She crossed her arms over her

chest, standing across from where I was trying to line up my shot first with just my right eye open, and then only my left. When I tried the two together, a wave of dizziness made me list to the side.

"Remember that night I saw Doc and Tiffany in the parking lot behind his office," she started, "and I thought they were back together?" At my cautious nod, she continued. "I went home to nurse myself back to happiness with Humphrey Bogart."

I decided to stick with my right eye for the shot. "I love Bogart."

"No shit, Sherlock. Anyway, I called you later that evening and told you I was going down to Doc's office and throw myself at his feet, but you stopped me. You convinced me to meet you here instead and then poured tequila down my throat kinda like tonight."

"Tequila is made from the agave plant, which had four purposes for the Aztecs." I held up four fingers, staring at them as I ticked them off. "Food, drink, clothing, and writing stuff."

"Thank you, Mr. Peabody, for your brainiac answer. Anyway, my question for you, Violet Parker, is: Were you with Doc when I made that call? Truth?" She held out a shot glass. "Or drink?"

In spite of my two shots of tequila, I knew exactly where I'd been that night when she'd called and it wasn't at home knitting a scarf for homeless chickens. I'd been in Doc's back room enjoying some naked time with him on a beanbag. If memory served me right, there was also a bottle of wine involved and multiple moments of breath-stealing pleasure.

I stared at her for several silent seconds while the jukebox switched songs. "Give me the damned shot." I held out my hand.

She chuckled. "Oh, how the mighty fall."

I followed her lead, downing the shot without salt or lime to ease its path. Unlike Foreigner and their "Hot Blooded" woes now filling our ears, my third shot went down without any heat. At least none that I felt anymore.

*Toot-toot*, the tequila train was now up to full speed.

I set the glass upside down on the table and pointed my pool cue at her. "Now, it's time for me to school you on how to play drunken eight ball, you tequila-guzzling harlot."

# Four Tequila

*An unknown amount of tequila-inspired trash talking later …*

Tequila was a slippery devil. One minute, I had the tail by the donkey. The next thing I knew, it'd bucked me out of the saddle.

"I have a question for you," I said, handing my pool cue to Natalie.

She frowned at it. "Why are you handing me that?"

"I'm passing the baton."

"What's that have to do with a question for me?" She took the pool cue from me.

"No, it's my turn to ask the question."

"Are you already tequila fried?"

"Truth," I answered, picking up my last shot glass and taking a sip. "No, but I'm getting close to tequila toasted." As in my face was numb, but my brain wasn't gone yet. "Now it's my turn."

She put both pool cues down on the felt and leaned her hip against the table. "Ask away, Calamity Violet."

"Truth or drink? Did you really sleep with that no-good bitch's boyfriend back in high school?"

"By 'no-good bitch' you mean your sister?"

I nodded. "Remember how she bragged about making out with that guy I was sleeping with? You know, the one with the Tom Selleck mustache?"

"You weren't sleeping with that one."

"I wasn't? Oh, you're right." I thought so anyway. The

tequila haze made it hard to see that memory straight.

"But you planned to on the next date."

"Oh, yeah." I glared down at the shot glass in my hand. "I had big plans."

"Yes, you did. But Susan slept with him first."

"She beat me to the plunge, the whore." I took another sip of tequila to wash that acrid memory down.

"Or something like that." Natalie hopped up on the side of the pool table, her legs dangling over the edge. "I didn't sleep with Susan's boyfriend, but I did make out with him behind the concession stand."

"Because he was hot?"

"No, because someone needed to retaliate. You were too busy crying in your pillow when the opportunity arose."

"He told Susan you two had sex."

She laughed. "In case you hadn't noticed, he liked to tell tall tales. But I let him talk because I knew how much it would piss off Susan."

"You ruined him for her." I smiled about it, too. "He dumped her after that but never explained why."

Her eyes sparkled. "Well, I might have told him that she had a chronic genital rash that the doctor had not been able to find a cure for yet, so he should be careful where he stuck things."

I covered my mouth. "Oh, you're bad," I said from behind my hand.

"Like I said, someone needed to retaliate." She tossed down what was left of her fourth shot in one gulp. "I had your back. I always have. That's why it hurt so much when you stabbed me in mine."

I winced. Even in my three shots of tequila liquored-up state, I still felt that blow. Guilt filled me, burning hot in my cheeks. I deserved worse.

"My turn," she said. "Truth or drink? During all of those times you messed around with Doc when I was still trying to win him for myself, did you ever think that maybe if you'd just told me the truth about falling in love that I would've happily stepped aside and let my best friend since forever have at him simply because it was you?"

I downed my shot, needing the courage to say what no longer could be avoided. I joined her up on the edge of the table. Or tried to anyway.

She hauled me up by the arm, steadying me when I teetered. "You sure you should be this high off the ground?"

"Shush." I swung my legs next to hers. "I'm going to tell you the truth and nothing but the truth, so help me God."

"You're not on trial, numbnuts."

After poking her in the ribs, I cleared my throat. "Natalie, I cannot change the past or my stupidity when it comes to what happened with Doc. There were many times when I wanted to tell you what was going on. Believe it or not, I even tried to break it off with Doc a few times."

"You *tried*, huh?"

"Yes." My voice rose in emphasis. "I really did. But when it came down to it, the pull was too strong. I wanted what Doc had to offer."

"The sex?"

"Not just the sex, although that was pretty …" At her deepening frown, I took a different tact. "Pretty, um, nice. I mean, you know, for a dried-up, desperate old mom like me who hasn't been with a guy for a long, longggggg time."

"Please. We're talking about Doc, whose ex-girlfriend is crazed with jealousy over him now sharing your bed. The guy oozes sexuality just standing in the grocery store line."

I stared at her, all hints of humor gone, needing her to understand why I'd done what I'd done so we could fill in this pothole before it grew any bigger. "You're right. The sex is great. The man has a magic touch. But it wasn't just the physical stuff with him. I've been with good-looking guys before, but from the start, Doc was different. I can't define how. Even after I found out about his ghost radar dealio and thought he was kind of crazy, I still wanted whatever crumbs he'd throw my way. He was like that missing edge piece I'd been looking for all of these years to make my puzzle border complete."

She snorted. "That's corny. Have you had your nose buried in romance books again?"

"Happily-ever-afters go well with bubbles, hot water, and wine, I'll have you know."

Her legs swung next to mine. "It's so embarrassing." She covered her eyes with her hands. "Doc must have thought I was a total tramp with the way I threw myself at him."

"No." I started to shake my head and then thought better of it, gripping the edge of the pool table for stability. "From the start, he wanted me to tell you the truth. He didn't like keeping you in the dark, but I was too much of a chicken shit. Me, not him. He thinks you're a wonderful person and a great friend."

She peeked out through her fingers. "Be honest—first kiss?"

I sucked up the courage and let the truth rip. "During the initial walk-through tour of his house in that narrow stairwell off the kitchen."

She lowered her hands. "First time you had sex?"

"In the back room of his office the day after the Hessler fire."

"How long did it all go on before I found out?"

I thought about that, hard, but that answer involved some math. "I don't know, Nat. My brain is soaked with tequila."

"A rough estimate."

"Two months." I threw out a number that felt right

even though what I'd done was all wrong.

She looked down at our swinging feet. "You should have told me, Violet."

"Yes. I'm so sorry. I was a huge idiot. My only defense is that I was terrified of losing your friendship."

"Our friendship is too old, deep, and full of sordid secrets to throw away over a man, Violet. But next time—"

"There will be no next time. Doc is the one."

Her eyebrows rose. "The *one*, huh?"

"The only." I leaned into her, bumping shoulders. "I hope."

She reached out and squeezed my hand. "Me, too."

"It scares the shit out of me, though."

"As it should."

"He holds my heart in his hands." I held my palms out, pretending to cup the beating organ that Doc now owned.

She gently tugged on one of my blonde curls. "If he gets one scratch on it, babe, I'll tear him to ribbons."

I let out a giggle hiccup. "It's your turn, you know."

"Okay," she said, pausing to take a breath. "I was stupid."

"Like your normal level of stupidity or like super-duper stupid with extra helping of dumbass?"

"Kiss my dumbass." She hopped to the floor and paced in front of me, wringing her hands.

"Let me help you get started," I said. "It was a dark and stormy night."

"It was dark, and Coop was definitely feeling stormy."

"Imagine that, and he didn't even know me yet."

She paused to look down at her hands, wiggling her fingers. The tequila must finally be working its magic. "Anyway," she returned to pacing, "I was here at the Purple Door wallowing in my beer after a long day of clearing brush behind my grandpa's place in Nemo."

"Why were you wallowing?"

"I was feeling lonely and the last few guys I'd dated had turned out to be real letches."

"You do have a way of scooping up slime balls from the bottom of the barrel."

She stopped pacing. "Do you want to hear the story or not?"

I mimicked zipping my lips.

"I was sitting at the bar working on my second beer when Coop walked in."

"What was he wearing?"

"Does it matter?"

I closed one eye, focusing on her with my less blurry one. "It helps me picture the scene better."

"I don't know. Jeans and a black T-shirt, I think." She crossed her arms over her chest. "Can I go on now?"

I gave her a crooked thumbs-up.

"He came over to the bar and sat down next to me, ordering a drink of his own."

"Beer?"

"Whiskey on the rocks."

"His usual."

She nodded. "I'd read in the newspaper that he'd returned to Deadwood, taking the job as detective, so I asked him how things were going."

"You knew him from school, right?"

"He was a bit older, but yes, I knew of him. I didn't figure he remembered me, but I was wrong."

"Of course he remembered you, he's a detective. His mind is a steel ball surrounded by rusty razor wire that's draped with hand grenades like deadly Christmas ornaments."

"You're regressing more than usual."

"I blame the agave plant."

"Anyway, I was flattered that he knew who I was. After all, he was James Bond hot, even when we were younger."

"He has the memory of two elephant brains wired together."

"Shut up and listen, you lush." When I did as told, she continued. "When he asked why I was drinking alone on a Friday night, I told him that I was working through some crap. He proposed shooting pool with him to help work off steam."

"What steam?"

"I don't know. His job-related steam. I didn't ask for details, just followed him back here and started shooting pool while I was still drinking. At first, neither of us had much to say, but after a few games and more drinks, we started joking around. That's when the flirting cranked up."

"Cooper flirts?" I played dumb. "What's that even like? Does he bare his teeth at you and growl a lot, pawing at the ground? Or does he sniff you up and down, and then pee on you?"

She laughed. "Believe it or not, he was a really smooth flirter, very talented at light touching and heated glances that made my pulse race."

"No shit?" The flirtatious attention I'd witnessed Cooper giving Natalie as of late could in no way be labeled "smooth." He seemed to stumble over words enough to make me squirm along with him.

"No shit. It started with a few compliments about my pool-playing skills, then moved to my hair, then my eyes. But rather than comment on my rounder parts to the south, his attention seemed to remain focused up north, asking me about tricks of my trade."

"What was his angle?" I asked, always a skeptic when it came to the detective.

"No angle, you cynic. I'm telling you, he actually listened when I explained the difference between dovetails and dados."

I blew a raspberry. "Everyone knows the difference

between ducktails and ..." What had she said again?

"*But* every time he thought I was focused on taking a shot, he was undressing me with those steely gray eyes. The subtlety of it all was a huge turn-on." She rubbed her arms, stopping to stare at the pool table, apparently lost in the past. "I made the first move, but not until after a couple of more beers. It took extra alcohol to get up the nerve to climb the wall he keeps built up around him."

"You've made the first move on plenty of guys while cold sober." I knew that for a fact, having witnessed it front and center.

"Plenty?"

"Well, a few at least."

"Yeah, but Coop was different."

"Because he could arrest you?"

She pointed at me. "That's your hang-up about him, not mine."

Whatever. "Different how?"

"Different like a panther, sitting up high, watching the jungle floor, waiting for the right moment to pounce."

"You've been watching *The Jungle Book* too much with Addy."

"We share a deep love for King Louie and his dancing."

"So what did you do for your first move?" I pressed. "Kiss him?"

"I hugged him."

I guffawed. "Well, that's not very sexy."

"He'd told me that he was offered a position on the other side of the state and was debating on taking it. I told him that they would be lucky to have such a great detective and gave him a hug partly because I was getting good and tipsy, like now, but mostly because he'd really cheered me up. I felt sad about him leaving town, and that wasn't just the beer talking."

"So you hugged him. That's snoresville stuff, you

know."

"What did you expect? That I wrapped my legs around him and rode him like he was a bucking bronco right here on the pool table?"

I wrinkled my upper lip. At least I thought I did. My mouth was now operating as a free agent, no longer ruled by my brain. "I just thought there was more touching involved."

"I'm not done with my story, Miss Impatience."

I leaned back on my hands, blowing a curly strand out of my face. "I'm all hairs."

"You mean ears."

"That, too."

"Anyway, I hugged Coop. When I tried to step away, he didn't let go. Instead, he backed me up against the wall over there." She pointed at the spot near the door that led out to the back stairwell and alley.

Now we were talking! "What happened next?"

"He told me he was going to kiss me and if I didn't want him to, I should stop him before he made contact."

"Not the most romantic," I said, critiquing his style, "but at least he didn't drag out the cuffs."

"I probably would've let him cuff me if he had, especially after that kiss. It knocked me for a loop."

"I always figured Cooper's tongue had serrated edges."

"Only around you, my dear." She came back and hopped up on the pool table next to me again. "You sure you want to hear the rest?"

"Yes, although I'm going to pretend it's not Cooper in this story, but actually James Bond instead. Sean Connery was always one of my favorites."

"Fair enough and I know all about your longtime lust for Sean." She rubbed her palms over her thighs. "Coop started the kiss real slow, sort of tasting me, you know. Teasing me with his tongue and feathery touches while he was at it. Everything inside of me pretty much melted from the heat building between us. Then he really cranked up the flames, pinning my arms over my head while he pressed his body against mine. The man is made of granite, I swear."

"I knew it! He's all jagged edges and craggy cliffs."

"I think you and I are thinking of two different kinds of granite. I meant south of the neck. Rock hard. Everywhere."

I grimaced, but kept my unflattering thoughts to myself.

"When he pulled back to give me a moment to catch my breath, he apologized about being too rough, saying he'd been wanting to do that since he'd walked in and seen me sitting at the bar. I told him I liked it rough and wanted more. Without another word, he hauled me out through the back door into the alley and pulled me into the shadows."

She looked over at me, her brow furrowed. "Is this too much detail? I know you're not his biggest fan."

"I'm drunk. I have a force field around here." I made a circle motion around my head. "I can handle it."

"You asked if there was red-zone touching."

I nodded.

"Yes, with a capital Y, E, and S. There was a lot of red-zone touching on both of our parts. His hands were everywhere, under my shirt, inside of my bra, stroking and teasing the whole time. Then his mouth followed, turning me inside out with love bites up and down. The nips he gave me on my hip bone and lower were nearly my undoing. I'd never had a man use his teeth on me like that before. The blast of pleasure mixed with pain had me begging him for more, telling him to do things I'd normally be too embarrassed to whisper even while I was drunk. When he did them, I completely lost it."

I tried to keep my expression void of winces and grimaces. *Sean Connery. Sean Connery. Sean Connery* was the chant in my head as she continued.

"Then it was my turn, exploring under his clothes, scratching down his back and over his chest." She stared down at her hands. "And then I moved lower, delving further into red-zone territory, touching, kissing, biting, giving back as good as I'd gotten." She blew out a whistle. "Damn, he was so hard."

"You already said that." I cringed on the inside. *Sean Connery*, I reminded myself.

"He made me feel like a million bucks," she continued as if I hadn't interrupted, "all the while saying things in my ear that had me reeling, ready to let him do whatever he wanted to right there in the alley like a cheap, drunken floozy." Her laugh was harsh and self-deprecating. "It wasn't one of my more respectable moments."

She paused, staring off toward the back door.

"Well?" I prompted. "Nosy ears are waiting to hear the end of your sordid tale."

She shrugged. "One minute we were tearing at each other's clothes, and the next his cell phone rang. Work was calling, even though it was his night off."

"But he'd been drinking."

"They said they'd send a unit to come get him."

"So he didn't reject you just to be a jerk." That put an end to that theory I'd had about their night together.

"No, but he could have told them to have someone else go check out what I learned later was just a prowler sighting." She sighed. "You know Cooper. His job always comes first."

"How come you never hooked up again after that?"

"Because he called me later that night, explaining the situation about the prowler. When I asked him to come over and finish what we'd started behind the bar, he told me that what had happened was a mistake. Then he apologized for being so forward and explained that he doesn't date local girls, end of story."

"Did he actually say 'end of story'?"

She nodded. "That still chaps my hide, too. That along with the impression that I left in the wake of it all."

"What do you mean?"

"I really like Coop, and not just because he's sexy as hell and made of steel. We had a good time that night even before the kissing started, talking and laughing. He treated me with respect. He didn't try to touch me inappropriately until I gave the green light and he didn't make rude comments about getting me in the sack like so many guys I run into here and down at the Blue Moon in Rapid. But because of that one back-alley moment with him where I let down my guard, he now undoubtedly thinks that I'm a slut."

"Nat," I started, deciding to tell her the truth about Cooper's renewed feelings for her.

"I'm serious, Vi. I hadn't had anything close to back-alley sex before that, nor since. There was just something about Coop and that night that had me willing to give him whatever he wanted and then some, my dignity be damned."

I gave her a sideways hug. "You need to stop beating yourself up. Cooper was just as willing as you, it sounds like. Does that make him a back-alley tramp?"

She shrugged. "It's different for guys."

"Maybe you should tell Cooper the truth about that night. Explain that it was a first-and-only time for you."

"It doesn't matter. He doesn't like local girls."

I begged to differ, but I focused on helping to rebuild her self-esteem via another route. "Maybe it would make things less awkward for you when he's around if you were to come clean about it."

"Does it show how uncomfortable I still am about it all?"

"Every now and then."

She rubbed the back of her neck. "I can't help it. That whole 'end of story' makes me want to take a swing at him with my hammer. It's not fair. He took control of what had fired up between us and doused it, not giving me a choice in the matter."

"That's very Detective Cooper–like of him."

She laughed. "You're right."

I tried inching into the truth. "Do you ever wonder if he might be interested in picking up where you two left off that night?"

"No. I think he made a command decision over his emotions and locked the door on me, keeping me safely on the other side." She kicked her feet for a few seconds. "There's no way I'm going to open that door again. I learned my lesson. He's dangerous for me both here," she pointed at her head first and then her heart, "and here."

I understood that danger full well, only I'd let Doc in and now there was no ousting him without a shitload of tears and a broken heart.

"Besides," she continued, "I'm on a sabbatical now. Me and my heart are feeling great and I don't want to rock the boat any time soon."

Well, that was that. Telling her about Cooper pining over her was not on the docket for tonight.

"I miss sex." She hopped down off the table, stumbling a little before catching herself. "But nobody ever died from not having sex."

Sex, no. A broken heart, maybe.

"Now, you know the rest of the story," she said in her impression of the late, great Paul Harvey. She held her hand out to me. "Enough talk about boys. Let's get some margaritas, crank up the tunes, and play another game of pool."

I hadn't realized the music had stopped. Her story had handcuffed me and held me prisoner, much like the damned detective who'd lit her on fire and then dumped a bucket of ice over her head.

I took her outstretched hand, same as I always had since we were little kids, and joined her for more fun and merriment. Only this time, we poured tequila into the mix.

# Just One More …

*One or two margaritas later … who's counting?*

Tequila was a slippery devil—wait, did I say that already?

I lined up my next pool shot, closing one eye to keep the balls on the table from moving so much. "Nine ball over there," I slurred.

"Over where?" Natalie asked and tittered, a sure sign that she was now officially well over the Tipsy state line. Wasted-ville was up around the bend.

"I'll show you." I took the shot, but none of the balls moved. I stood up frowning. "I think I missed."

She danced over to me, sloshing her second margarita along the way. "You missed the cue ball completely. Move over and let me show you how it's done."

I took her drink, stealing a sip of salty-sweet margarita goodness.

Natalie leaned over the table so far that she was half lying on it. She lifted one leg, wiggling further along the table top. What was she going to do? Hit the cue ball with her nose?

Something moved on my right. I swung my chin in that direction and frowned at the bristly detective standing next to me.

"Uh, Nat," I said in a stage whisper. "I smell bacon."

"I swear, woman," she said without looking back, "you are addicted to that meat."

I stumbled closer to the pool table. "I'm talking about Smokey Bear." Still nothing from the woman cueing up. "The Heat. Wyatt Earp. Barney Miller. Columbo."

Natalie tossed aside the pool stick cue, using her middle finger instead. She tapped on the cue ball with her fingertip.

"Barney Fife," I said, no longer whispering.

She rolled onto her side, frowning up at me. "You forgot Starsky and Hutch. That old red and white Ford Torino really lit my fire."

I waved her off, almost falling over in the process. "The General Lee could take that Torino in a heartbeat."

"Give me that," Cooper said, stealing Natalie's margarita from me. "You're going to dump it all over the table."

Nat's gaze shifted to my right. "Hey, Vi, why didn't you tell me the fuzz is here?" She tried to sit up a couple of times and then gave up and held out her hand. "I need a boost."

Before my brain could figure out how to get a message to my hand, Cooper was there helping her to her feet. He leaned her against the table and then looked us both up and down. "Christ, you're both completely wasted, aren't you? Nyce is going to owe me double for this."

"Where's Doc?" I asked, looking around the bar. Wasn't he supposed to be playing cards with Cooper?

"He's waiting outside at the curb, keeping the car warm while I drag you two drunks out of here."

"Ahhh, isn't Doc so sweet," I murmured to nobody in particular.

Natalie crossed her arms over her chest. "Lay off, Coop. It's my birthday."

The detective caught Natalie as she started to tip to the side, holding her steady as I scrambled up onto the edge of the pool table, falling off twice in the process.

"I need to lay down for a minute," I told the eight ball.

"We need to go, Parker. Not take a nap."

I lay back on the table, grunting as a pool ball dug into my kidney. "I need to wait for the room to stop spinning first."

"Are you okay to walk?" he asked Natalie.

"Yep, but I'm not going anywhere without Vi."

I smiled up at her. "You're such a great best friend. I love you so much."

"I know," she said and tittered again. When she stopped, she fanned herself. "Damn, it's hot in here tonight." She lifted up her sweatshirt, pulling it off over her head. Her pink satin camisole fit her like a second skin.

"What are you doing, Natalie?" Cooper asked, his eyes widening in surprise as he took in her half-undressed state.

"I'm hot," she told him, climbing up on the table and lying back next to me. "Wow, the stained glass isn't as pretty from this view."

"I know, right?" I reached up toward it, letting the light outline my fingers. "Do my fingers look longer to you? I think they're growing as I get older."

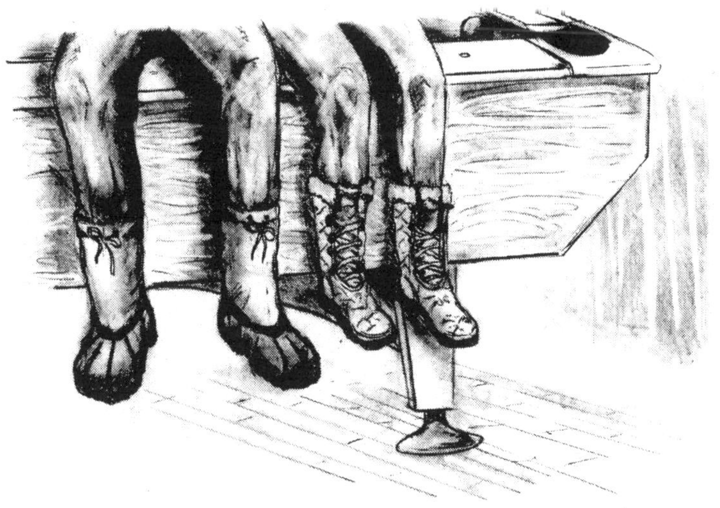

"Fuck," I heard Cooper mutter. "Come on you two, before I have to arrest you for being drunk and disorderly."

Natalie turned her head, grinning at me. "Coop is very bossy."

"I noticed."

"But he's still sexy."

"Sure, if you like to juggle chainsaws and swallow fire balls."

Cooper grabbed Natalie by the upper arms and hauled her upright. "Put your sweatshirt back on, Beals." He held it out to her.

"Make me, Officer Cranky Pants." She held her wrists out toward him. "Or handcuff me and throw me in jail."

I struggled up onto my elbows. "She's wearing a camisole, so you can't arrest her for public nudity, *Coop*."

"That's Detective Cooper to you, Parker."

I wrinkled my nose at him.

"Listen, Coop," Natalie said, pulling free of his hold and sliding off the table and onto her feet. "You need to understand something here."

"What's that?"

She pointed at her chest. "I'm not a slut."

I frowned, trying to follow her train of thought, but the tequila made the rails slippery.

One of Cooper's blond eyebrows lifted. "I never said you were."

She crossed her arms over her chest, making her breasts puff up under the lacey edge of her camisole. "When I offered to have sex with you back there that night," she said, gesturing with her thumb toward the door, "I was breaking one of my top five rules when it comes to men."

His gaze narrowed. "Which rule was that?"

"Never have back-alley sex with a hot cop."

The corner of his lips twitched. "That's actually one of your rules?"

"Sort of." She huffed. "But now you think I'm some tramp who will let any guy screw her on the first date."

He shook his head. "That's not true."

"I'll have you know, Detective," she continued, poking him in the chest, "I have slept with only five men in my life." She held her hand out with all five fingers extended. "Vi here has a much more visited vagina than me."

"Say what now?" I sat upright.

"So you can take your 'end of story' bullshit, Coop, and sit on it!"

Oh dear, she'd regressed to silly lines from her Fonzie fangirl days.

"Because I'm not some barfly who you can get your kicks off with and then dump like a cold turkey. I have feelings, too."

He stepped closer to her, lowering his voice. "Why did you go with me into the alley that night, Natalie?"

She shrugged. "You made me feel special."

"You *are* special."

"And desired?"

"I wanted you more that night than I've wanted any other woman before or since."

Had he really said that out loud? I looked at Natalie, trying to see how she took that.

"But you made it clear how you feel about me," she continued, apparently not really hearing his replies. "*End of story, Beals,*" she imitated his growly voice. "Don't worry, I'm not going to throw myself at you again, Detective. I just wanted you to know that I'm not easy."

"Good."

"And you'll be happy to hear that what happened that night between us won't *ever* happen again."

"That's not the news I wanted to hear." He reached out and snaked her hand, pulling her toward him.

"What are you doing?" she asked, trying to tug free as

he reeled her closer.

"Parker," he said without looking my way, "close your eyes."

By the time his words registered in my tequila-addled brain, he was kissing my best friend.

I stared wide-eyed at the scene, trying to comprehend that what was playing out in front of me was really happening.

His hands cupped her cheeks, holding her steady as he slowly brushed his mouth over hers, coaxed her lips open, and then kissed her until she moaned. Her hands climbed up his chest, her fingers spread wide. She arched into him, like she was ensnared and towed closer by some invisible force.

He drew away, groaning her name as he stared down at her. Even in my drunken state, I could hear the deep hunger in his low voice.

Natalie blinked up at him, her mouth open as she leaned toward him again. Then she seemed to snap out of his spell and pushed away, backing into the pool table. "What are you doing, Coop?"

His gaze was still locked onto her lips. "The story isn't over."

"Huh?"

"You heard me." His focus lifted to her eyes. "I'm sorry, Natalie."

"For what?"

"Treating you poorly. You deserve better." He reached out and stroked her cheek, as if she were a delicate flower petal. "I'm going to do it right this time."

"This time?" I repeated, earning a shooting glare from the detective.

He turned back to Natalie. "Stay right here. I'll be back with Nyce to help carry you two out of here."

Then he was gone.

I blinked, shaking my head slowly, feeling shocked. I turned to my best friend. "Wow! Did you see that?"

Natalie frowned at me, touching her lips gingerly with her fingertips. "Was Coop here a moment ago?"

The tequila made the details hard to remember. "I think so."

"Did he kiss me or is the tequila fucking with my head?"

"Yes."

"That explains why my lips are burning." She leaned her hip against the table. "Did I act like I enjoyed it?"

"The tequila or the kiss?"

"The kiss."

I scrunched my forehead, replaying the end of the scene in my hazy brain. "You didn't throw up in his mouth."

She cringed. "Well, that's good."

"What do you think we should do about Cooper?" That question was actually supposed to stay inside my own head. Should I tell Natalie the version of the truth about Cooper wanting to handcuff her to his headboard indefinitely?

"Nothing," she answered, sitting next to me on the table.

"Really?" I didn't think Cooper was going to like her answer.

"I'm on sabbatical, remember? Besides, I learned my lesson last time I got too friendly with Coop's lips."

"Once bitten?" I put my arm around her.

"Twice burned." She leaned her head on my shoulder and sighed, sounding like a lovesick groupie. "But hell's bells, that cop knows how to kiss a girl senseless."

The End … for now

## Sneak Peek Alert! (Shhhhh…)

Join me in the Yucatán jungle for a sneak peek from the second full-length novel in the Dig Site Mystery Series, *Make No Bones About It*, starring Quint Parker (Violet Parker's brother) …

***Muan*: A screech owl. In Maya iconography, the *muan* is often linked with rain, maize, and the Underworld.**

"How deep in shit am I?" Quint asked as he secured himself into the helicopter's passenger seat.

His old friend Pedro Montaña held out an aviation headset for him. "When I left the dig site the day before yesterday, *mi ángel* was sharpening her machete. That was before she knew I was going to be delayed an extra day, along with her supplies. I didn't dare let her know I was waiting for you to fly in."

Damn it. Angélica was probably breathing flames by now.

Settling the headset over his ears, he stared out the windshield with a frown while Pedro performed a pre-flight check. The Mexican jungle was lying in wait for him at the edge of the tarmac. Somewhere, amidst the trees and bugs and critters, the woman he'd obsessed about for the last several weeks was waiting to chew him a new ass.

Razor-sharp machete or not, Quint couldn't wait to see her again.

Pedro spoke a few words into his mic to the traffic controllers, and then they were lifting off. They rose above the trees, flying over the thick green sea of canopy broken only by a spider web of roads. Pockets of small towns popped up here and there, as well as clusters of gray stone structures left behind by the ancient Maya.

Since his last visit to this humid hellhole, Quint had spent his spare time during his photojournalist travels practicing his Spanish and learning about the Maya people and their leave-behinds. After his crash course, his head still spun when it came to all of their gods and beliefs, but if he were going to try to win Angélica's affection for the long haul, he'd need to start with that big brain of hers. As soon as he'd gained a foothold on her logical side, he'd work his way down to her heart.

"We have visitors." Pedro's static-laced voice came through the headset, interrupting Quint's thoughts about the flame-haired Dr. García, who was undoubtedly waiting to breathe fire all over him for his tardiness. Not to mention his lack of communication.

Visitors? "At the dig site?" he asked Pedro.

Quint hadn't been able to get through to Angélica or Juan since he'd left Cancun, thanks to his own clumsiness while floating along in the north Atlantic. He'd pulled out his phone to check his messages during the boat ride to the remote village where he was to spend a couple of weeks photographing polar bears for an article in a well-known nature magazine. But thanks to his frozen fingers, the phone had slipped from his hand, bounced off the railing, and splashed into the icy water.

With the sinking of his phone went the only number he had for Angélica, which made for many long, dark, lonely nights of shivering in his sleeping bag, reliving heated moments under the Mexican moon in an effort to keep warm. Acclimation was a bitch when traveling from steamy temperatures to freezing … and back to steamy. He grimaced and wiped at the sweat coating his forehead. Luckily, he'd had a few days in between to defrost at home in South Dakota before returning south again.

"You know what INAH is?" Pedro asked.

"Yeah." It was the branch of the Mexican government in charge of archaeological sites. And the people in charge of Angélica's career at the moment.

Pedro glanced his way. "They have brought in five crew members to pay for the ... what's the word Juan used to make it sound nice ... the *pleasure* of working with us."

"Pay? You mean INAH advertised the open field crew positions?"

Quint had heard of this practice before for grad students in anthropology and archaeology programs. If memory served him right, they applied to be "hired" at a particular dig site. After being accepted, they paid a chunk of money, traveled on their own dime to the site, and worked their asses off in exchange for college credits, lousy food, and uncomfortable beds. Finding a dig site with modern plumbing was an even more expensive proposition, of course.

At Pedro's nod, Quint asked, "Did Angélica have a say in any of this?"

"No. She was allowed five of her own crew. INAH picked the others."

He grimaced. The boss lady must be gnashing her teeth about that. "Are these five new crew members already on site with her?"

"*Sí.* She and Fernando have been training them."

Babysitting, in other words. Something she'd had to do with Quint at her last site. He could imagine the range of curse words flying from her sweet lips as of late.

So Fernando was back. Juan had explained to him when they'd worked together before that Fernando had been acting as Angélica's foreman since she'd taken over as lead archaeologist after her mother had died. Quint enjoyed working with Fernando, who shared a love for María's *panuchos* along with a mutual loathing of Angélica's ex-husband.

He stared down through the window at a tour bus traveling along one of the roads that wound through the Maya lowland forest. "Who else from the old crew has returned?"

"Teodoro and María, of course. INAH counted them as one instead of two, since they don't actually do field work."

They were more like support crew. Quint smiled out the window about the couple being there. Just thinking about Teodoro's homemade *balche*, a sacred, honey-based Maya drink, made Quint's mouth water. The inebriating effects might come in handy when it came to softening up Angélica after his longer-than-promised absence. Of course, María's cooking would keep them fat and happy while they sweated buckets and battled the flies and mosquitoes all the livelong day.

"Esteban agreed to come back."

Good ol' Esteban. Quint chuckled under his breath, remembering some of the snags the boy had gotten himself into at the last site. Angélica's choice to include Esteban made sense. While he might be scared of his shadow and often tripped over his own feet, she had mentioned once that the clumsy Maya youth was extremely smart and very trustworthy. On top of that, his father was disabled, so Esteban was the sole moneymaker for his family. Angélica might be rigid when it came to her rules on her dig site, but for her crew, she'd bend over backward to help them. "Who else?"

"Lorenzo, her *padre*, and me."

"So you're not volunteering your services this time?"

"No. Angélica pulled some ropes and managed to get me paid for flying in her crew and supplies, as well as working on site."

*Ropes?* He must mean she'd pulled some strings. Pedro was fluent in English, but that didn't stop him from mixing up his metaphors and screwing up his idioms.

"That's why I waited for you, although you're not officially on the payroll as one of the crew. All INAH needs to know is that I was delayed picking up supplies."

Quint didn't want to be on Angélica's official crew, taking valuable monies out of her budget. He'd aligned a paying job again through another archaeology magazine, a follow-up article about Angélica and her father's progress after his last piece covering their work.

Having been in the business for almost twenty years, Quint's contact list was long and landing a quick gig filling magazine pages in between contract jobs usually took only one or two calls, especially when the main focus of the piece involved two current stars in the Mesoamerican archaeology arena.

"So, who are these five new crew members?" he asked Pedro. "All college students?" Who else would want to pay to work among snakes, spiders, and man-eating mosquitoes?

"Three of them are students. One is an older lady, very pretty, probably in her late fifties. The other is a writer, like you, only he has no camera. He's here to do research."

Quint's brow tightened, suspicion bubbling in his gut. Another journalist? Who'd sent him and why? Someone out to get the dirt on Angélica now that her ex-husband had made the news? Someone hired by a rival archaeologist to knock her off the pedestal on which the Mexican government had her placed at the moment?

Juan had once told him that Angélica not being born in Mexico was a black mark on her record as far as the government was concerned, so she had to work extra hard to keep her job with INAH. Being female wasn't doing her any favors either in what had been a male-dominated profession until recently.

"Is this writer working for a magazine or a newspaper?"

"Neither. Maverick writes books about monsters."

"A fiction author?"

Pedro nodded. "A cowboy from Nevada."

A cowboy who writes about monsters? "What's his pseudonym?"

"'Maverick' is all he has said so far. I can't remember his last name. You know how Anglo names go in and out of my ears."

"Maverick," huh? Quint wasn't convinced this so-called author wasn't hiding a devious truth behind his reason for visiting a pest-infested Mexican jungle. "What's a fiction author doing on a Maya dig site?"

"Research. He wants to write a story about us."

That must have gone over with Angélica like a cement blimp. She hated letting anyone handy with a pen on her site. Not having a say regarding what was written about her and her father's work made her hair practically crackle with sparks.

Quint knew that from first-hand experience. She'd tried to throw him off her last dig site multiple times. Unfortunately for her, he was as stubborn as she was when he had his mind set on something he wanted. And he'd really wanted answers to a twenty year old mystery, along with some more alone time with a certain curvy archaeologist.

They flew along in silence for several minutes, Quint trying to think of all the fiction authors he'd read or heard about online or at airport bookstores. No "Maverick" came to mind. That had to be part of a pseudonym, didn't it? He'd never met anyone actually named Maverick.

He glanced at his watch. They were fifteen minutes from the site. He'd find out first-hand about this fiction author soon enough.

Below them, the tree canopy seemed to be growing thicker with fewer roads and villages to break up the greenery.

"Tell me about this new dig site," he said to Pedro. "From what I could see on the map, it's practically nonexistent."

The internet hadn't been much help, either. There had been several articles on the neighboring biosphere reserve that had been set aside years ago by the Mexican government, but nothing with the site name Pedro had mentioned when Quint had called him two nights ago.

"It's in the middle of nowhere and full of bugs and animals."

"What kind of bugs are we talking about?"

"Really big bugs." Pedro chuckled at Quint's curses.

"Monkeys, too," he added, "and birds, snakes, rats, cats, deer, tapir. You name it, this place has it."

"Did you say cats?"

"Ocelots, puma, margays, and jaguars. They mostly come out at night."

"Nocturnal hunters."

"Exactly. The sound of their growl in the dark is enough to make you piss yourself, and when they roar, your *cojones* shrivel up into teeny tiny raisins."

"Holy shit. We're like a buffet line." Quint grimaced down at the jungle below. Why in the hell had Angélica chosen this damned site?

"When you go to the bathroom in the night," Pedro continued his tale of horrors, "hundreds of spider eyes shine back at you."

"Christ." All of this for a woman? What was wrong with him?

"I have a light I use to find the scorpions. I'll let you borrow it. They like to hang out around the latrine."

He must mean a black light. Quint shuddered. Truth be told, he didn't think he wanted to know what was out there waiting for him. Ignorance might be bliss on this trip. Then again, with venomous snakes on the loose and hungry cats, this adventure could be the death of him.

"Did you bring earplugs?"

He'd learned long ago in his travels to always keep a pair in his shaving kit. "Sure. Why?"

"The noises in the night make it hard to sleep at first."

"What noises?"

"You'll see. I sleep with a pillow over my head most of the time."

"I can hardly wait to experience this Mexican paradise."

"It's good that you cut your hair."

Quint had purposely had the barber trim it shorter than usual to help him keep cooler.

Pedro gave him a toothy smile. "It will be easier to remove the ticks each night."

"*Each* night?" He scratched his head, suddenly feeling little phantom bodies crawling all over his skull. "Jesus, Pedro. Is there anything good about this damned site?"

"Besides your *novia* waiting for you there?"

"And her sharp machete."

"María is probably cooking as we speak."

"Food is definitely good."

"There are lots of butterflies and bats."

Butterflies were great. Maybe he could put together an article on butterflies for one of the popular nature periodicals. Bats were bug eaters, and if there were as many mosquitos as there had been at the last site, they'd need all of the bats they could round up.

"We have cleared a spot for our tents and the shower."

"Where are you getting water?" Were there *cenotes* this far south?

"There is a small stream nearby and several springs. We also brought in a few cisterns."

"How many tents are we talking?" At the last site, there had been enough for most of the crew to have their own quarters.

"*Cinco*."

"Only five?"

"Plus the mess tent. We are sleeping in pairs, except for the three female INAH students—they share one of the bigger tents."

"Couldn't INAH spring any extra money for more tents?"

"It's not about money, it's about safety."

Safety? "Is Angélica worried about the wildlife attacking?"

"It's not *mi ángel* who's scared."

"What do you mean?"

"Her *padre* is not happy about being at this site."

"Because of the snakes, rats, and scorpions?" Juan had a severe dislike for vermin, especially those with sharp teeth, stingers, or venom.

"This is the site that killed his wife, Angélica's *madre*."

Quint did a double take. "Marianne died here?"

"The helicopter taking her away from the site crashed after takeoff. She died in the hospital from her injuries."

Quint knew the story. He'd heard bits of it from Juan and Angélica both. "Why would she want to come back here?" he said to himself as much as to Pedro.

"Marianne left something in her notes about a certain stela with some important glyphs."

"Not another curse," Quint said jokingly.

"Yes, a curse."

His jaw gaped. "You're kidding me."

"No joke. Juan says it is a curse. Angélica says it's a warning, not a curse." Pedro shrugged. "Until they find the stela Marianne wrote about, nobody knows for sure."

Son of a bitch. "Another curse." Quint scoffed. "What are the chances?"

"Very good. The Maya were very superstitious."

Silence followed, broken only by the thump-thump-thump of the helicopter blades and the high-pitched whine of the engine. Quint pondered Angélica's choice in sites. What good was being here where her mother had met her end? She couldn't bring Marianne back.

Was this so-called curse the appeal? No, Angélica didn't believe in curses. She was too down-to-earth for that. It had to be something her mother had written. Some theory she needed to prove to put her mother's ghost to rest? That was what had made her hell-bent for leather at the last site.

"I agree with Juan." Pedro broke the silence.

"You think it's a curse?"

He nodded. "But not a supernatural curse, more like bad juju."

"Why? Because Marianne died?" What about the other archaeologist? The previous crew? Had anything happened to them?

"Not because she died. Because of *the way* she died."

"You mean the crash?"

"Exactly. It shouldn't have happened. I have an old friend who works for the government. He is part of a team that investigates aircraft crashes, like Marianne's."

Pedro had mentioned this friend previously when talking about Dr. Hughes' plane crash years ago. "Was it pilot error?"

Pedro shook his head. "The official ruling was that a pitch control rod in the main rotor failed. Mechanical failure was listed as the cause of the crash."

"You think the curse had something to do with that?" Quint had trouble believing a curse could cause a mechanical failure.

"According to my friend, a rod failing like it did is highly unlikely. However, his supervisor and the government wanted to be done with the crash investigation, so they swept it under the floor. 'Mechanical failure' was the final ruling. So, either there was a curse at work, or someone wanted Marianne dead."

Who would have wanted her dead?

Pedro added, "You must promise not to talk about this around Angélica and Juan."

"Of course not." What good would come of that? It would only open old wounds better left scarred over.

"You are an ace detective, right?" Pedro asked.

He grimaced. "Not really an ace." His style was more bumbling gumshoe with a shitload of luck mixed into the deal.

"You and I will work together in secret and find out the truth." It wasn't a request, more of a statement.

"You mean if Marianne was murdered or it really was some ancient bad juju?"

"Yes. And if it was murder, we will figure out the killer, because whoever was responsible might decide to kill her daughter, too." He frowned over at Quint. "We don't want to see that happen, do we?"

"Hell, no."

Pedro pointed down at the trees. "That's the site."

A small clearing amid the trees sat below them. Located only a short distance from several crumbling gray stone structures was a group of army-green tents.

Quint mulled over Pedro's words as they began their descent. They'd almost reached canopy level when something slammed into the helicopter's windshield and then ricocheted up into the blades.

Feathers flew.

Pedro cursed in rapid-fire Spanish.

"What was that?" Quint asked, peering up through the windshield.

"Very bad news."

"What do you mean?" The helicopter seemed to be unharmed.

"It was a screech owl." Pedro shot him a quick frown. "A *muan*."

"What's a *muan*?"

"The evil bird of bad tidings."

"Seriously?"

"It's a sign."

Of course it was. "Of what?"

"*Yum Cimil*, or as some call him, *Ah Puch*. The lord of death, ruler of the ninth level of the Maya underworld."

According to the book Quint had read on Maya gods and religion, the Underworld was the Maya version of hell. "And a *muan* is his pet bird?"

"Not a pet, a messenger." Pedro craned his neck, checking the landing area as the ground loomed beneath. "When you see or hear a screech owl, someone will die," he said as he set the helicopter onto the grass with a soft bounce.

"And what about when you chop it up in the blades of your helicopter?"

As the engine wound down, he turned to Quint, his brow wrinkled. "I'm afraid to find out."

***Make No Bones About It*, the second book in the Dig Site Mystery Series, will be available in March 2017.**

Ann Charles is a USA Today Bestselling author who writes award-winning mysteries that are splashed with humor, romance, and whatever else she feels like throwing into the mix. When she is not dabbling in fiction, arm-wrestling with her children, attempting to seduce her husband, or arguing with her sassy cat, she is daydreaming of lounging poolside at a fancy resort with a blended margarita in one hand and a great book in the other.

Facebook (Personal Page):
http://www.facebook.com/ann.charles.author

Facebook (Author Page):
http://www.facebook.com/pages/Ann-Charles/37302789804?ref=share

Twitter (as Ann W. Charles):
http://twitter.com/AnnWCharles

Ann Charles Website:
http://www.anncharles.com

96936507R00048

Made in the USA
Lexington, KY
25 August 2018